Adventures with Sister Philomena,
Special Agent to the Pope

CURSE
OF THE COINS

Written by DIANNE AHERN

Illustrated by BILL SHURTLIFF

Aunt Dee's Attic, Inc.

Adventures with Sister Philomena,
Special Agent to the Pope:
CURSE OF THE COINS

Copyright 2008 Aunt Dee's Attic, Inc.

A Book from Aunt Dee's Attic

Published by *Aunt Dee's Attic, Inc.*
415 Detroit Street, Suite 200
Ann Arbor, MI 48104

Printed and bound in Italy

Library of Congress Control Number: 2007902200

ISBN 978-0-9679437-7-0

1 2 3 4 5 6 7 8 9 10

First Edition

www.auntdeesattic.com

This book is dedicated to the Patrons of the Arts in the Vatican Museums and to the artists and artisans who restore its treasures.

Special Thank You and Acknowledgments to . . .

. . . the staff of the office of the Patrons of the Arts in the Vatican Museums, including Father Allen Duston, OP, Father Mark Haydu, LC, Giovanna Bortolamedi, Sara Savoldello, and Gabriella Lalatta,

. . . Father Jeffrey Njus, Pastor of St. Thomas the Apostle Catholic Church, Ann Arbor, and Rome aficionado, for his review with respect to Church teachings,

. . . the proofreaders, editors, and reviewers who came to the aid of the author, including: Lisa Renee Tucci, Josiah Shurtliff, Shiobhan Kelly, Leo DiGiulio, and LeAnn Fields,

. . . Jillian Downey for the work on the text layout and design,

. . . the people who shaped the story, including Delaney and Riley Miner, Angel and Cielo, Keenan Allion, Timothy and Sheri Marotz and their children Christian, Zachary, and Meghan.

Other books by Dianne Ahern:

BOOKS ON THE SACRAMENTS:
Today I Was Baptized
Today I Made My First Reconciliation
Today I Made My First Communion
Today Someone I Love Passed Away
Today We Became Engaged

ADVENTURES WITH SISTER PHILOMENA,
SPECIAL AGENT TO THE POPE SERIES:
Book 1: *Lost in Peter's Tomb*
Book 2: *Break-in at the Basilica*

CHAPTER ONE

THE SISTINE CHAPEL

"That's Adam and Eve in the Garden of Eden," explains Riley, pointing to one of the pictures painted on the ceiling of the Sistine Chapel. It's early morning in the Vatican, and Riley and his little sister, Delaney, have been left alone to explore the Sistine Chapel while their aunt meets with the Pope. Pictures called murals and frescos cover every inch of the walls and ceiling. It looks to him like a picture-Bible had exploded inside the chapel and plastered the stories of God and Jesus and Moses and the Apostles and Mary and Adam and Eve and popes and saints and angels all over every surface.

"Do you see the snake wrapped around the tree?" Riley asks his sister. "That snake is really the devil. And it's telling Eve to eat the fruit from that one tree— after God told her and Adam they could do anything in the garden *except* eat the fruit from that tree. It was forbidden! But Eve was tempted by the devil and even convinced Adam it was okay to eat the fruit from the tree. And so they went ahead and followed the devil, disobeying God. That was wrong, *really* wrong! Even worse than not listening to Mom or Dad, or to Aunt Philomena. Afterwards Adam and Eve were kicked out of the garden."

"How come they don't have any clothes on?" asks Delaney.

"Because it was the beginning of creation and clothes hadn't been invented yet. Adam and Eve didn't need clothes at first, because they lived in paradise and in paradise you don't know you're naked. But after they disobeyed God, they realized they were naked and they wanted to cover themselves up. At first they used fig leaves to make clothes. The fig leaves didn't last long, so I think they experimented with feathers and animal skins."

"Humph," replies Delaney, squinting her eyes so she can see better. The ceiling is very high, and the pictures seem very far away, but oddly, from way down here on the floor, the people in the pictures seem normal-sized. "Are you sure?" she asks her brother. Delaney just graduated from kindergarten and knows a lot of things, but there are still things she is unsure about. Since her parents aren't around this summer to ask, she has to trust what her older brother and their aunt tell her. She is just not sure whether or not to believe Riley on this one.

"How did they paint all those pictures way up there on the ceiling?" asks Delaney.

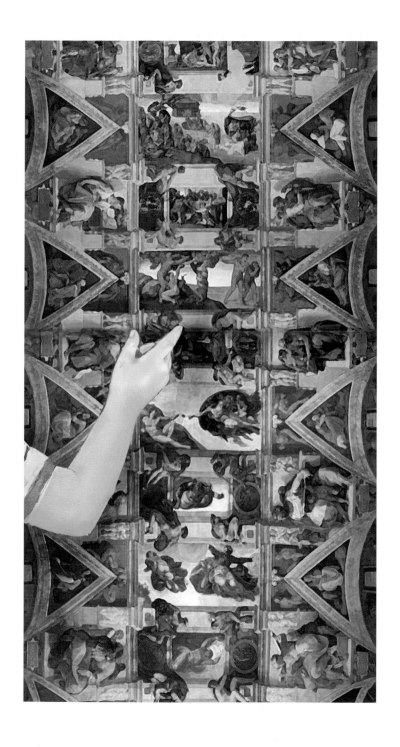

"Good question," responds Riley, flipping through the pages of a small guidebook. "Let me read a little further in this book Aunt Philomena gave us. If I can't find the answer, we'll ask her. She'll know. She knows everything!"

Riley and Delaney are spending this summer in Italy with their aunt, Sister Philomena. Their home is in the United States, but after the school year ended they came here with their parents, who have business meetings with agricultural leaders in other parts of Europe. Their mother and father thought that it would be more interesting for them to spend the summer in Italy with their aunt than to stay home with a nanny—even if it meant being the only children staying in the convent all summer.

What their parents did not know is that Sister Philomena, their mom's sister, in addition to being a nun, is a special investigative agent for the Pope. When the Pope needs help with an investigation regarding the Church or church property, he relies on the skills and talents of Sister Philomena; she is the Pope's number one investigator.

When they first arrived at the convent, which is in a small town near Rome named Grottaferrata, Riley worried that this was going to be a dreadful summer. What was a guy like him supposed to do in a convent with a bunch of nuns? He was certain that all nuns did all day was pray and go to church. He just knew he was going to die of boredom. Most of all, he was afraid his friends back home would find out that he had spent the summer in a convent, and would never let him live it down.

But now he can't wait to tell his friends about his adventures this summer with his aunt. So far this has been the best summer of his entire life. His aunt has taken him and his sister all over Italy to investigate crimes and find lost artifacts; they have visited the ancient Roman Coliseum, the tombs of emperors and Christian martyrs, churches and basilicas filled with art; they've been to hill towns, cities, and even remote villages. A lot of interesting things have happened. Sometimes, he and Delaney have been scared out of their wits, and sometimes they've gotten lost. However, the fact that their aunt lets them help with her investigations makes up for all that.

The convent isn't at all the awful place that Riley had imagined. The other nuns are kind and fun-loving and enjoy teaching him and Delaney useful Italian words and phrases. Mostly, the sisters in this Order are gardeners, growing grapes, olives, and vegetables. They make the wine used for Consecration during Mass in the Vatican and at other churches in Rome. True, they do go to church and pray a lot—but that's not *all* they do.

Earlier this morning, Sister Philomena was called to the Vatican once again to meet with the Holy Father about something he wanted her to investigate. That's all she was able to tell Riley and Delaney before she sent them off to the Sistine Chapel with a guidebook.

Normally, children their ages would not be allowed in the Sistine Chapel or elsewhere in the Vatican without an adult with them. The Vatican is the home of the

Pope, and the famous Saint Peter's Basilica, Saint Peter's Square, the Vatican Gardens, a fantastic museum, and the Sistine Chapel. An ancient brick wall surrounds the Vatican, and Swiss Guards dressed in brightly-colored uniforms and carrying big bayonets stand watch at every entrance to keep people from going where they shouldn't.

When they first started coming to the Vatican, Riley and Delaney were allowed to sit in on their aunt's meetings with the Pope. But Delaney got too fidgety and always interrupted. Now when Sister Philomena

and the Pope meet, Delaney and Riley are sent to the Vatican Museums, the Sistine Chapel, or Vatican Gardens. The Museums are filled with pictures, statues, tapestries, the Popes' carriages, ancient maps, Etruscan treasures, and so much more. They're fantastic! However, when the Museums are crowded with other visitors, the children go to the Vatican Gardens to play. The Vatican Gardens are almost as big as their farm back home, and are a treasure of plants and flowers, statues, fountains, grottos, and meandering walkways. The Gardens are a great place to play hide-and-seek.

Over time Sister Philomena has learned that the children will usually stay out of trouble if she gives them a guidebook and an assignment to learn something new about the Vatican. This morning, their mission is to study the ceiling of the Sistine Chapel and to give her a report.

"What are they talking about?" questions Delaney as she continues to stare up at the dozens and dozens of pictures painted on the ceiling.

"Who?" asks Riley, thinking she's asking about the people in one of the pictures. Riley scans the ceiling, and then pokes around in the guidebook, but he can't seem to find a picture of people talking.

"Aunt Philomena and the Pope. They've been gone a long time. We should try to find them," insists Delaney, as she sits up to look at her brother.

Just then, their aunt comes rushing into the Chapel. "Come along, children, we have a job to do!" she says excitedly.

Sister Philomena has learned to take advantage of her niece and nephew's remarkable talents. Riley seems to be a budding detective—kind of a "chip off the old block," she thinks proudly. He has an inquiring mind and is very smart.

Delaney on the other hand has a keen eye for detail and a genuine appreciation of art. If you ask her to describe the scene in a painting, she can usually figure out what the artist wants you to see, and can explain it to you. Sister Philomena has enjoyed showing Delaney a lot of new art, especially religious art, since she and her brother came to Italy.

"Two pretty terrific kids," she thinks to herself, and then smiles quietly as she ponders the new assignment that the Pope has given her. She also wonders how she will keep the children out of trouble while making the best use of their talents. Then she worries that she might be placing them in danger in trying to solve this latest puzzle.

CHAPTER TWO

THE MISSING COINS

"This way, children," Sister Philomena urges as she ushers Riley and Delaney through the door to the office of Father Allen, the Director of the Patrons of the Arts in the Vatican Museums. The Patrons volunteer and raise money to pay for the care and restoration of all the works of art that are kept by the Vatican Museums.

"We can use Father Allen's office to make a few phone calls before we start our assignment. I need some time to get organized and to study a letter that was sent to the Holy Father."

"What assignment? What letter?" asks an impatient and very curious Riley as he plops down in an enormous arm chair on the opposite side of the desk from his aunt. Father Allen's huge desk is made of dark wood and looks ancient, just like nearly everything in the Vatican. The legs and sides of the desk are carved with flowers, leaves, and figures that look like angels. Riley has to sit on his feet to make himself tall enough to see his aunt's face on the other side. Delaney has decided to crawl around on the floor so that she can study the figures carved into the legs of the desk.

"I might as well tell you now," confides Sister Philomena, "you will need to know sooner or later anyway. It seems that someone has stolen a set of very valuable coins from the laboratories of the Vatican Museums. The coins were sent here from Israel for authentication; that means to make sure they are for real and aren't fakes. The person or people who sent the coins remains a real mystery. But the museum staff were told that these particular coins are believed to be the actual thirty pieces of silver that were paid to Judas when he betrayed Jesus."

Riley gets a quizzical look on his face.

"Do you know the story of Judas' betrayal of Jesus?" asks a concerned Sister Philomena. "It comes at the beginning of the story of the Passion of our Lord Jesus Christ."

"Tell us the story! Please?" begs Delaney as she crawls out from beneath the desk and climbs up onto Sister Philomena's lap.

"The Passion story relates the events of Jesus' sacrifice on the Cross that took place around the year 33 A.D.," begins Sister Philomena. "Jesus was returning to Jerusalem after convincing hundreds of thousands of Jews and gentiles to repent of their sinful ways, to look to God as their Father and LORD, and to love one another. Some of the Jewish leaders at the time became jealous of Jesus and wanted Him out of the way. These leaders—primarily the priests and Pharisees—saw that a lot of people had come to believe that Jesus was the Son of God and were following Him. This bothered the leaders, as they were afraid that they would lose their important jobs if people turned away from the Jewish faith. The Jewish leaders knew that the Roman soldiers would be angry if someone was calling himself the "king" because the Romans wanted everyone to bow down to their king, King Herod, who was the king of the Roman Empire at that time. So, the Jews told the Roman soldiers that Jesus was proclaiming himself to be the King and they insisted that the Roman soldiers go find Jesus and punish Him.

"Earlier in His ministry, Jesus had selected twelve apostles to go out and preach the news of repentance, forgiveness, and salvation. Judas was one of those twelve apostles, but he turned out to be a traitor. When Judas learned that the Roman soldiers were looking for Jesus so they could arrest Him, he decided to turn Jesus over to the soldiers in exchange for thirty pieces of silver.

"It was in the evening after the Passover meal, what we now refer to as the Last Supper, that Judas led the Roman soldiers and some of the Jewish leaders to the place where Jesus was staying—the Garden of Olives. The Bible tells us that the Apostle Peter was there with Jesus, as were the Apostles John and James. Judas had agreed to lead the soldiers and Jewish leaders to Jesus, and when they all arrived at the Garden of Olives, Judas went and gave Jesus a kiss on the cheek. This was the signal they had agreed he would use to identify Jesus. The Roman soldiers then captured Jesus and led Him away. Afterwards, the Jewish leaders paid Judas his thirty pieces of silver. Often when you see Judas depicted in the artworks around here, he is shown with a bag of money in one of his hands. Perhaps before you go to bed this evening you can read about this in your Bibles—it's in the Gospels of John, Chapter 18, and in Matthew, Chapter 26.

"Jesus was placed on trial by the Roman officer Pontius Pilate. An angry crowd of Jews and Romans demanded that Jesus be found guilty. Then the Roman soldiers took Jesus, put Him in prison, crowned Him with thorns, tortured and tormented Him, made Him carry a heavy wooden cross through the streets of Jerusalem, and finally crucified Him on Calvary. These events are all part of what we call the Passion of Christ.

"After Jesus died on the cross, Judas was consumed with guilt. The thirty pieces of silver were like poison to him. He went back to the Jewish temple and hurled

the coins at the priests and Pharisees. Then Judas went away and hung himself.

"The chief priests gathered up the thirty pieces of silver that Judas had thrown at them, and it is reported that they said '*It is not lawful to deposit this in the temple treasury, for it is the price of blood.*' Instead, they decided to use the money, the coins, to buy the potter's field for use as a burial place for foreigners. You can read about this in Matthew, Chapter 27.

"Throughout history, everyone assumed that the owners of the original potter's field took the thirty pieces of silver and spent them like any other coins of the time.

"However, last month in Jerusalem, the Franciscan Friars at the Church of the Holy Sepulcher found a leather pouch with some very old silver coins inside—thirty coins to be exact. Whoever sent the coins put a note inside the pouch indicating that they think the coins are cursed, because over the centuries, the families who have had possession of these coins have been wicked.

"The Friars didn't know what to do with them. In fact, the Friars were afraid to keep the coins. Instead, they sent the coins here to the Vatican for safekeeping and for authentication by the laboratory staff of the Vatican Museums. But before anyone could examine the coins, they disappeared.

"Earlier today, a letter about the coins was sent to the Holy Father by courier. Whoever sent the letter claimed that he or she knows the whereabouts of the missing coins. The note instructed the Holy Father on what he needed to do in order to get them back."

"A ransom note?!" Riley asks, clearly excited.

"No, it wasn't really a ransom note—it seemed more like a cry for help. I have a feeling that whoever wrote the note is desperate. I think it sounds like a plea to solve a puzzle."

"Can we help solve the puzzle?" Riley persists, now intrigued by the case. The skin on his arms has turned to goose bumps thinking about these ancient coins, their link to Jesus, and the possible adventure that lies ahead.

"Both of us?" wonders Delaney, as she twists around in Sister Philomena's lap to look her squarely in the face.

"I guess so," Sister Philomena laughs quietly. "You know that I can't leave you alone either here in the Vatican or back at the convent. Besides, we have worked so well as a team this summer on other cases that I couldn't think of starting this one without you. Come, let's look at this letter."

TO:
VATICAN
MUSEUM

HANDLE WITH CARE

THE PUZZLE

Sister Philomena carefully opens the letter sent to the Holy Father and lays it on Father Allen's gigantic desk. Father Allen's office is in the part of the Vatican that was built around 1500. Ironically, here at the Vatican, they call it the "new section" since it's *only* 500 years old! The floor is red stone tile and the walls are lined with old, rich-looking wood paneling. Some of the wall panels actually hide secret closets and passageways. The office was once part of the private apartment of Pope Innocent X, who was pope from 1644 to 1655. Riley wonders what kind of people visited this room way back then, who knew about the secret passageways, and what kind of dealings took place here so long ago. The room is filled with an air of history—and mystery—and that makes the start of this investigation even more exciting.

"Please, read it to me?" pleads Delaney. Delaney hasn't quite learned to read yet and the words she sees are confusing to her.

"Hmmm," ponders Sister Philomena. "The letter is written in Italian, but the use of words makes me think that the person is not fluent in Italian. My, my, this is very curious."

"What does it say? Translate it for us!" Riley and Delaney sing out together. Sometimes they can be very impatient.

Sister Philomena reads the letter out loud in Italian:

"Andate prego al posto delle teste Decapitate. Troverete un sacchetto delle monete. Avrete bisogno di una scala. Cercate un' altro indizio."

"It starts off by saying *'Go, I pray,'* but a more traditional translation would be, *'Please go.'* It appears that our puzzle was written by a polite person," observes Sister Philomena.

"Translated literally it says:

"Please go to the place of the decapitated heads. You will find a bag of silver coins. You will need a ladder. Look for another clue."

"Now what do you suppose our mysterious puzzle writer is trying to tell us? It's strange that the "D" in *decapitate* is capitalized. That's not proper Italian." Sister Philomena rests her chin between her thumb and forefinger as she assesses the situation.

"What's de-capittulated mean?" asks Delaney.

"It means a head that has been chopped off the body, like with a guillotine!" adds Riley excitedly.

"Yuk!" exclaims Delaney.

"Well, in this case, I believe it refers to a head or skull that has been removed and preserved as a relic; or perhaps a sculpture of a head or the head of a statue," cautions Sister Philomena. "There are dozens of decapitated heads in Rome—as relics, I mean. Certainly not fresh ones!"

"We've seen bones and skulls all over Rome!" gasps Delaney. "How can we tell which ones the puzzler's talking about?"

As they have been visiting the sights of Rome, Delaney has been surprised that almost everywhere they went, they found themselves looking at, or standing on top of tombs of people who lived in ancient times—some dearly departed pope or saint or even an ordinary citizen.

Sister Philomena smiles at Delaney, thinking of all the things she has seen this summer that are unusual for a girl her age to experience, and how well Delaney is coping with all of it.

"Let's look at the second sentence," suggests Sister Philomena. "It's pretty clear. It says 'You will find a bag of coins.' After all, that's what we're after. We want to retrieve the thirty pieces of silver. So when we find the right decapitated heads, we should find the coins.

"But the next sentence seems to be a key clue. It says... 'You will need a ladder.' I would have expected the puzzler to ask for some sort of payment for the coins; that he or she is holding them for ransom. Ransom is where a thief demands money or valuables in exchange for whatever it is that the thief took. But in this case the ransom for the coins surely isn't a ladder. That just doesn't make sense. Maybe it means 'You will need a ladder to climb up on something.' Let's think about this. Where in this city would somebody need to climb on a ladder in order to see decapitated heads?" ponders Sister Philomena.

"Well, how many important people are there here who got their heads cut off in Rome?" questions Riley.

"Saint John the Baptist!" offers Delaney, excitedly. "And, there's a humungous head downstairs in the courtyard beside the Museum entrance."

Riley is amazed that his sister remembered the beheading of John the Baptist, and wonders how she thought of that. Sometimes she's hard to figure out. After thinking about this for a minute he says, "I don't think John the Baptist was in Rome when he was beheaded. And that head in the courtyard is a bronze sculpture—you can climb on it but you don't need a ladder. Think of someone else.

"Maybe the puzzler is telling us there is a connection between the coins, the decapitated heads, the Pope, and the… I don't know what. Were the heads of any of the Apostles cut off in Rome?"

Sister Philomena paces back and forth for a while and says, "Riley, you surely do have detective blood in your veins. You might have 'hit the nail on the head,' as they say."

"They should say, 'hit the nail on the decapitated head!'" chuckles Delaney, trying to make a joke. Riley rolls his eyes.

Sister Philomena smiles and shakes her head. "Well, there is a basilica here in Rome where the heads of the Apostles Peter and Paul are said to rest. The name of it is the Basilica San Giovanni in Laterano. In English it's called the Basilica of Saint John Lateran. In this basilica, above the high altar, is a reliquary made of solid gold. It kind of looks like a big golden cage. Inside the gold cage are two life-sized male figures, also made of

gold. Inside the gold bodies supposedly rest the skulls of the Apostles Peter and Paul. This gold cage is very high up above the altar and you would definitely need a ladder—or several ladders—to reach it. Hmmm," Sister Philomena says, trying to fit the pieces together.

"Let's go take a look," says Riley impatiently. "How far away is it? Can we walk there?"

"We could walk, but it is pretty far. We'd be better off having a driver take us there and then asking him or her to wait nearby while we search the basilica. That way, if we don't find what we are looking for in the Basilica of Saint John Lateran, the driver will be able to take us somewhere else and we won't have to wait for a taxi or a bus."

"Can we use the Pope's car?" asks an excited Riley. Riley just loves riding around in the Pope's big, black, chauffeur-driven car. It makes him feel really important.

"No," says Sister Philomena. "The Pope is using the car today. He's leaving this afternoon for his summer residence in Castel Gandolfo. His driver and the car will be stationed there with him. You know, sometimes the Pope gets to use the car himself!"

"I'll call the convent to see if Sister Lisa Renee can come and drive us around Rome," says Sister Philomena. "She should just be returning from her summer retreat at Lake Como and should be available to help us out."

Riley and Delaney turn towards each other with scared looks in their eyes. They know all about Sister Lisa Renee.

CHAPTER FOUR

THE HUNT BEGINS

Riley stands watch at the window of Father Allen's office for Sister Lisa Renee, who is expected to arrive any minute. She drives a little car with sun-bleached red paint and with dents and scratches all over it. The car belongs to the convent, but Sister Lisa Renee is the only person who dares to drive it. Riley knows from previous adventures that Sister Lisa Renee drives like a crazy woman. He was surprised when his aunt told him that of all the sisters in the convent, Sister Lisa Renee is the safest driver, as she has never had an accident. Riley wonders where all the dents in the car came from, in that case. And being the best driver among a bunch of nuns isn't necessarily a great achievement. Still, the fact that she drives in Rome with all the other crazy drivers and has never had an accident is nothing short of a miracle.

Suddenly, the little red car comes careening into the private courtyard below Father Allen's office. Riley watches as Sister Lisa Renee hits the brakes and brings the car to an abrupt stop. When she turns off the engine it makes a chortling sound for a few seconds, then lurches forward, and finally comes to a stop with a loud bang and puff of blue smoke. Sister Lisa Renee lays on the horn. Frightened pigeons scatter in every direction. Two Swiss Guards come rushing into the courtyard, waving their hands in a downward gesture to try to quiet the honking horn. Riley laughs as he sees Sister Lisa Renee putting her hands to her mouth as if to say, "Oops! Sorry for disturbing the peace."

Sister Philomena grabs the black valise that Riley immediately recognizes from earlier investigations, and hurries the children down the wide marble stairs and out into the courtyard. The Pope uses this marble stairway and courtyard when he comes and goes, and so do VIPs coming to the Vatican to visit the Pope. Riley knows from personal experience that the Swiss Guard keeps constant watch over this courtyard for security purposes. He hopes Sister Lisa Renee hasn't gotten them in trouble with the Swiss Guard by honking the horn.

As Riley, Delaney, and Sister Philomena arrive in the courtyard, they see Sister Lisa Renee standing beside the car, admiring the towering granite columns and walls of the buildings that surround her. *"Mamma mia,* this place is awesome!" she gasps.

The Swiss Guards seem to be focused on something in the back seat of Sister Lisa Renee's car. When Riley sees the amused looks on their faces, he stops worrying that the Swiss Guards plan to arrest her for disturbing the peace. As he, his aunt, and sister approach the car, they hear a piercing howl, followed by a round of barking.

"Where did you get them? Are they yours? What are their names? Can we keep them?" Riley and Delaney pepper Sister Lisa Renee with questions. Sister Philomena frowns in disbelief as she peers into the backseat.

"I'm sorry," explains Sister Lisa Renee. "I brought them with me from our retreat house in Lago di Como, Lake Como. I was driving home from there when I got your call. One of the sisters staying at the retreat house this week has allergies, so I brought them with me. I didn't want to take the time to drop them off at the convent in Grottaferrata before coming to get you. If I had done that, it would have taken hours for me to get back here.

"I love you!" coos Delaney as she opens the car's back door and pulls out a little black, white, and tan beagle dog. She pets his soft furry head and long ears. The dog, wagging his tail a thousand times a minute, begins to lick her face. Delaney giggles in delight.

A second beagle, a little larger in size, takes advantage of the open door and jumps out of the car. Not to be left behind, the smaller dog wiggles free of

Delaney's grasp, and suddenly the courtyard is filled with the sounds of yelping and laughter. The dogs romp on the cobblestone pavement, chasing each other and being chased by the Swiss Guards and children. The nuns watch with amusement, laughing heartily at the entire scene.

"*Viene qui, Angela,* Come, Angel! *Viene qui, Cielo!*" commands Sister Lisa Renee. "*Venite, sedete!* Come! Sit!" As she speaks these commands she reaches in the pocket of her habit and pulls out a couple of dog treats. The two dogs run up to Sister Lisa Renee, sit

right in front of her, and look intently at the hand that holds the treats. After rewarding the dogs she commands, *"Andiamo!* Let's go!" and the dogs jump back into the car, tails happily wagging.

What a scene! The two guards, two nuns, and two children look on in amazement as the two dogs that just caused such chaos in the Vatican courtyard now quietly sit in the backseat of the car.

"Sister, how did these dogs learn to be so obedient?" questions Sister Philomena.

"I've been training them all summer, and now they

seem polite enough to join our convent family,"
responds Sister Lisa Renee.

Sister Philomena smiles and teases, "You'll have to
get the okay from Mother Superior first. I thought that
my asking to have two children stay at the convent for
the summer was a lot to ask. Let's just see how far you
get with two dogs!"

The Swiss Guards, relieved that the dogs are now
safely contained, open the doors of the little red car,
encouraging the nuns and kids to climb inside. The
Guards, who are supposed to be prepared for almost
any security situation, joke that they should add "dog
chaser" to their list of security responsibilities.

As Sister Lisa Renee navigates the car out of the courtyard and through the gates that separate the Vatican
from the City of Rome, Sister Philomena tells her
about the stolen coins and the note. "I need you to
drive us to the Basilica San Giovanni in Laterano. You
can wait in the car with the dogs while the children
and I scout out the basilica."

CHAPTER FIVE

THE GOLDEN CAGE

Riley finds riding through Rome as exciting and interesting as ever. Emergency sirens wail and car horns honk. Compact cars and motor scooters speed along the streets, then slam on their brakes for pedestrians stepping out to cross the street. Although pedestrians in Italy are supposed to have the right-of-way at all times, Riley thinks that crossing the street on foot is way too dangerous, considering the way people drive. He's even noticed that cars don't always stop for red lights in Rome—so why would they stop for people?

Riley and Delaney sit in the backseat, each hanging on to one of the beagles for dear life as Sister Lisa Renee zigzags through traffic. The dogs keep shifting their weight back and forth to keep their balance. They, too, have ridden with Sister Lisa Renee before!

Sister Philomena has taken a small black notebook out of her valise and is trying hard to write legible notes in it as the car swerves back and forth. Riley is amazed at his aunt's calmness, especially as Sister Lisa Renee rants and raves at the other drivers and cars.

Riley wonders what his parents would think if they knew that he and Delaney were riding all over Rome in a car driven by nun who is a daredevil driver. They would probably be horrified!

"We're here!" announces Sister Lisa Renee proudly, as she parks the little red car halfway onto the grassy lawn in front of the huge basilica. "This is the Basilica San Giovanni in Laterano, or Basilica Saint John Lateran, for you English-speaking kids. This is *THE* cathedral of Rome. It's the Pope's home parish. You've heard the phrase, the 'Bishop of Rome.' Well, the Pope, in addition to being the Pope of the entire Church, is also the Bishop of Rome, and this is the cathedral of Rome. Before Saint Peter's Basilica and the Vatican were built, this was the place that the Popes called home."

A curious Delaney asks, "Who's up there?" as she points to the statues on top of the basilica. "They look like the ones over Saint Peter's, only a little different. How come they put statues on top of buildings in Rome?"

Sister Lisa Renee responds, "A long time ago, when they built these basilicas, they put statues up there to call attention to the importance of Jesus, the Apostles, and the Saints. Just look how big they are! The statue in the middle is Jesus, the risen Lord. On one side of

Jesus is a statue of Saint John the Baptist and on the other is Saint John the Evangelist. The other statues are of saints and Church fathers. I just love the feeling you get standing in front of this basilica. It's so big! So filled with faith!"

Riley and Delaney seem overwhelmed at the size of the basilica as they walk up the lawn with Sister Philomena. Five arches tower above them at the front of the basilica, below the statues. The basilica is so huge that the people sitting on the steps and standing in front of the arches look like little toy figurines placed in front of a real palace. Behind the arches is a long wide portico or porch. Huge bronze doors open into the basilica. The doors are so big that Riley wouldn't be surprised if it took two or three people just to push one of them open.

"Giants! Giants! Giants!" exclaims Delaney, taking hold of her aunt's hand and marching down the main aisle of the basilica. Delaney begins to count the statues. "Look at them all! One, two, three, four . . . ." Midway down the aisle she stops in front of the statue of Saint Thomas to study it in more detail. She notices his finger pointing up.

"These are the statues of the Twelve Apostles," explains Sister Philomena. "The first two by the door are Simon and Thaddeus. Then we see Bartholomew

and Matthew, James the Minor and Philip, John and Thomas, Andrew and James the Major, and finally, Peter and Paul.

Riley has been studying the names on the bases of the twelve statues. "So, Judas the traitor-apostle isn't here?"

"No he isn't," explains Sister Philomena. "There is no place of honor for Judas. Here, Saint Paul gets recognized as being the Twelfth Apostle. Although Paul was made an apostle after Jesus was crucified and rose from the dead, Paul is often included as one of the twelve."

"Is that the golden cage you told us about?" asks Riley as they face the main altar. High above are two figures made of gold with golden halos around their heads and golden vertical bars on all four sides that come together to look like a cage. Below the cage are beautiful pictures of Jesus and Mary, and above is a golden steeple with a cross on top.

"That's it," whispers Sister Philomena. "The skulls of Peter and Paul are supposed to be stored within the figures inside that golden cage."

"Are skulls the same as decapitated heads?" questions Delaney nervously, as if she isn't really sure she wants to know.

"Pretty much so—anyway, let's hope that this is the

place the puzzler was referring to in the note," says Sister Philomena.

Riley listens but seems a little doubtful about this explanation. "Do you really suppose the puzzler put the thirty pieces of silver way up there? How could he get them up so high? Look, even if I stand on your shoulders, and Delaney stands on my shoulders, we can't reach all the way up to the golden cage. I hope he didn't put the coins inside the skulls."

"Ewww!" cries Delaney, disgusted at the thought of putting anything inside a person's skull.

"I hope he didn't either," says Sister Philomena. "Maybe the puzzler just tossed them up there, or maybe he used a long pole. Let's just hope the coins are there."

With Delaney in hand and Riley at her side, Sister Philomena walks around the altar to size up the situation. "How can we get to the top? How did the puzzler do it? Is this really the 'place of the decapitated heads' the puzzler mentioned in the letter?" Many doubts begin to race through Sister Philomena's mind.

All of a sudden Riley spies a car-like object that maintenance workers use to reach the ceiling of the basilica tucked away in a shadowy corner. It has a bucket in which someone can stand, an electric car underneath for the driver, and a hydraulic lift that raises and lowers the bucket. "Look, I bet we could reach the top with that," Riley says excitedly.

"I am sure we could, but I don't know how to operate it," cautions Sister Philomena, stepping closer to have a better look at the controls.

"The bucket part of the lift would certainly hold one or two people. Look at all of these levers in the car part. One group must be used to drive the lift, and the other set of levers must move the bucket part up and down. They are pretty well marked, and the key is in the ignition."

Sister looks at Riley, Riley looks at his aunt, and they both have mischievous smiles on their faces.

"What if I drive it and you ride in the bucket, Riley? I could raise you up to the golden cage where the skulls are and you could look for the coins," says Sister Philomena.

"Cool!" exclaims Riley. He has that feeling you get when you are about to do something daring and a little dangerous. "Let's do it!"

"The challenge will be to do this without being noticed," cautions Sister Philomena, looking around at all of the people visiting the basilica.

Ring. Ring. Ring. Just then the sound of chimes fills the basilica, and people start heading toward one of the side chapels.

"Thank you, Lord," says Sister Philomena. Smiling triumphantly, she looks at Riley and Delaney. "It's time for Mass!"

"Wh-what?" stammers Riley in disbelief. "We already went to Mass at the convent this morning. You made us get up really early. Don't you remember? You aren't going to make us go again, are you?"

"No. But with that attitude, maybe I should," teases Sister Philomena. "The ringing of the bells gives us just the break we need. Everyone in the basilica will be going to the chapel for Mass, so we'll have the place to ourselves for thirty to forty minutes." Looking at the vertical lift she says, "Let's hope we can get this monster going without being noticed."

Riley climbs into the bucket of the lift while Sister Philomena sits at the controls with Delaney on her lap. Sister practices moving the levers that control the up and down movements. At first the motion is very jerky, and Delaney giggles as Riley grabs his stomach and moans in discomfort in the bucket. Sister then tests her skills on the back and forth controls. After a little practice, she is able to maneuver the lift quite smoothly.

After checking once more to be sure the coast is clear, Sister Philomena drives the lift over to the altar and activates the bucket, raising Riley high above the gold figures.

Riley peers out from the top of the bucket and says quietly but excitedly, "Holy smoke! This place looks really different from way up here."

"I'm sure it does," says his aunt in a loud whisper, "but you are not up there to sightsee! Please, just look for the silver coins."

"Nothing on this side," says Riley. "Drive me all the way around."

"What's that over there?" He points as they turn the corner to go around the golden cage. Looking across the basilica, Riley sees what appears to be a picture of the Last Supper. It is embossed in gold and sits high up above a side altar.

"Is that the Last Supper?" Riley asks, leaning over the side of the bucket so his aunt can hear him without shouting. "It looks like a picture that our priest back home showed us in my religion class once. Only this one is in gold!"

"Oh my, yes," confirms Sister Philomena, whispering quite loudly over the sound of the lift's engine. "I have to tell you that behind that golden replica of the Last Supper is a portion of the table that Jesus and the Apostles actually sat around during the Last Supper. It is among the most precious of relics, but few people know that it's here at the Basilica of Saint John Lateran."

A chill runs down Riley's spine as he realizes that he is this close to something that Jesus and the Apostles actually touched. He feels very lucky and really blessed.

"Hurry, Riley, keep looking for the coins," urges Sister Philomena. "Mass will be over soon and the tourists will be returning to the basilica. Look for something unusual. The coins could be loose, or they may be in a box or something."

"I see a little bag over there," Riley says, peeking through the bars of the golden cage. "I think the coins might be in it. Aunt Philomena, drive the bucket a little closer to the back so I can reach the bag."

In her excitement, Sister Philomena accidentally hits the "Up" button, skyrocketing Riley and the bucket clear up to the ceiling. Riley hangs on for dear life as she overcorrects her mistake and brings the bucket down too fast, nearly sending Riley flying out of the bucket.

A frightened Delaney screams, but the visitors attending Mass are singing and they don't hear anything. Sister makes the *Sign of the Cross* and thanks God that she didn't dump Riley out of the lift. Calmly she positions the bucket close to the spot that Riley had indicated.

"Got it!" cries Riley, as he snatches a little brown leather pouch from the corner of the cage and peeks

inside. "It looks like old coins all right, but I only see six. Wait, I see a piece of paper inside, too. Bring me down."

Just then the singing in the chapel gets a little louder. It's the final hymn. Mass will be over soon and the tourists will be back in the basilica. Sister Philomena must hurry and get the lift down and returned to the place where they found it. She parks the lift and turns off the engine without being noticed. But just as Sister Philomena is lifting Riley out of the bucket, a man's voice shouts at them from across the basilica. "What's going on over there?"

Turning, Sister Philomena sees a security guard hurrying toward them. In a surprisingly calm voice she explains, "Sorry, officer, the children were curious about this strange-looking car. I was just showing it to them. I don't think we hurt it. Shall we wait while you inspect it?"

Realizing that it is a nun he's talking to, the security guard relaxes. "Oh no, Sister, no problem. I am sure it's fine. You and the children have a good day." From the look on his face, it would be hard for him to imagine a nun doing something wrong. He seems embarrassed about having shouted at her.

Sister Philomena takes Riley and Delaney by their hands and rushes them to the door. "Do you have the leather pouch?" she asks Riley.

"Yes. It's in my pocket. That was close!" Riley replies.

Sister Philomena breathes a sigh of relief. "It sure was!"

"Now let's go find Sister Lisa Renee. Then we will need to find a quiet place where we can look at the coins and see what's on the piece of paper."

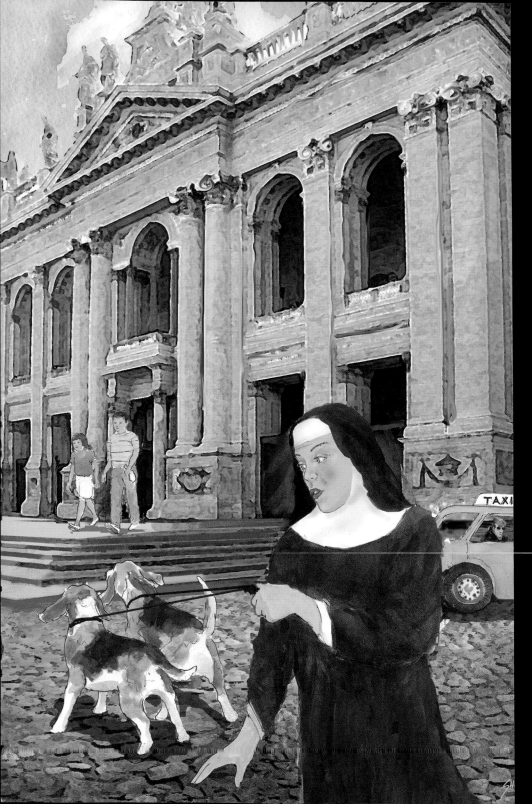

CHAPTER SIX

SCENT HOUNDS

Sister Lisa Renee and the two dogs have been walking along a grassy knoll beside the basilica. The dogs spot Riley and Delaney leaving the basilica and they take off running towards the children, dragging the nun along behind.

"Aunt Philomena and I drove a car up to the place where the heads are and lifted Riley up in a bucket and he found the coins!" blurts Delaney as she reaches Sister Lisa Renee. Sister Philomena realizes that Delaney will probably not grow up to be a good detective, because she has to tell everything. The dogs crash into the little girl and push her down. Delaney giggles with delight as the dogs insist on sniffing and licking her.

"You did what?" asks Sister Lisa Renee, staring at Sister Philomena and Riley with a look of bewilderment.

"It's a long story. I'll tell you later. Do you think you could keep Delaney and the dogs busy for a little while?" asks Sister Philomena.

"Absolutely," agrees Sister Lisa Renee. She has no interest in getting involved in Sister Philomena's investigations, no matter how interesting they might be. Sister Lisa Renee is a free spirit, like Delaney, and detective work would take way too much thinking! She says "Come on, Delaney, there's a park across the street where we can let the dogs run," and they take off running and dodging cars as they cross the street to the park. Neither of them seems the least bit intimidated by the traffic.

Sister Philomena turns to her nephew and says, "Riley, let's sit here on the grass where we can study the contents of the pouch." She takes a piece of white cloth from her valise and spreads it on the ground. Riley takes the mysterious leather pouch out of his pocket and empties it onto the cloth. The first things to fall out are six round, flat objects. Each one is imprinted on both sides, but the imprints are not even. One side looks like a head, the other like a bird of sorts. The disks are dull and tarnished and definitely look like they could be two thousand years old. It would not be hard to believe that these objects are, in fact, six of the thirty silver coins taken from the Vatican earlier today.

Then a crumpled piece of paper falls out of the pouch. It's folded, but unevenly—it's been scrunched up to fit inside the pouch. Sister carefully unfolds it and lays it on the cloth next to the coins.

"Is it a ransom note?" asks Riley.

Sister Philomena shakes her head. "I don't think so," she says, "it looks more like a poem or a rhyme. This note is as strange as the earlier one that was sent to the Holy Father. Only this time some of it is written in English." She reads out loud to Riley:

> *Once in royal David's city*
> *Stood a lowly cattle shed,*
> *Where a mother laid her Baby*
> *In a manger for his bed:*

Mary was the mother mild,
Jesus Christ her little Child.

He came down to earth from heaven,
Who is God and Lord of all,
And His shelter was a stable,
And His cradle was a stall;
With the poor, and mean, and lowly,
Lived on earth our Savior holy.

She quickly recognizes the words. "Why, that's a hymn that we often sing during the Christmas season. It is strange that the puzzler uses it in this way. It certainly is not Christmastime.

"Look here, the rest of the note is in Italian, sort of Italian anyway. It says,

Nella casa grande della Madonna hanno messo
la base del stalla.
È stato rubato o salvato stato?
Le monete d'argento sono rubate or salvate?

"My goodness, I think it says, 'In the big house,' that's *nella casa grande,* 'of the Madonna, there is put, or sits, the manger bed.' I wonder if the 'big house of the Madonna' could be the Basilica Santa Maria Maggiore. The word 'big' and *maggiore,* which means 'major,' could be confused. The Basilica Santa Maria Maggiore is one of the four major basilicas in Rome and is actually part of the Vatican. It was the first church ever built to honor Mary, mother of Jesus. Mary is called the Madonna. I see a connection between that and the rhyme or hymn, don't you?"

"Yes, kind of," says Riley, looking a bit confused. "But what about the manger? And what do *rubato* and *salvato* mean?"

"In Italian, *rubato* means 'stolen,' and *salvato* means 'saved,'" Sister Philomena explains. "I think it's asking if the manger in which the infant Jesus was placed was stolen or saved? Then the puzzler wrote, 'Are the silver coins stolen or saved?'"

"Wait a minute!" exclaims Sister Philomena. "Here in Rome there is a part of the manger from Bethlehem that is said to be the actual manger in which Jesus was laid after His birth. This most precious relic is actually *in* the Basilica Maria Maggiore."

"How did it get there? Is the puzzler asking if the manger was stolen or saved?" questions Riley. "Or is the puzzler asking the question about the silver coins—are they 'stolen or saved?' This is very confusing. Should we go to this basilica and look for stolen coins or a stolen manger?"

"Very confusing indeed," says Sister Philomena. "But yes, we must go to the basilica and look for both the manger and the coins. God forbid that anything has happened to the manger relic. Come, let's get Sister Lisa Renee to drive us there!"

The two nuns, two kids, and two dogs jump back into the little red car. Sister Lisa Renee starts the engine, coaxes the car into gear, eases out into the traffic, and then drives like she is playing "dodge-em" with the other cars on the streets of Rome.

During the ride, the dogs keep sniffing at Riley's pocket and trying to put their noses into it. The dogs seem to be after the pouch that contained the coins and the note. "What is the matter with them?" he asks Sister Lisa Renee. "Why do these dogs want to get into my pocket?"

"Angel and Cielo, *calma, calma,* calm down," Sister Lisa Renee commands from behind the wheel of the car. She adjusts the rearview mirror to see what's going on in the back seat.

"Riley, you have to realize, these dogs are scent hounds, sometimes used for hunting and for sniffing out smuggled goods at airports. Once they get a smell of something unusual, they are determined to find it. You didn't put any food in your pocket, did you?"

"No, just the leather pouch that I grabbed from the place with the heads."

"Stop that, it tickles!" Riley says, as he tries to push

the dogs away. The dogs keep coming after him and
the leather pouch. "Here, Aunt Philomena, you take it."

Riley tosses the pouch to his aunt in the front seat.
Suddenly the dogs leap over the seat and begin climbing all over the nuns trying to get at the pouch. Sister
Philomena takes the pouch and holds it up in the air
to keep it away from them. Her efforts are fairly use-
less, as the dogs jump up and claw at her arm, first
from the seat and then from her lap.

"Whoops!" shouts Sister Lisa Renee. She swerves the car to avoid hitting a pedestrian and then swerves sharply in the other direction to keep from running into a city bus. The car seems to be careening out of control. It grazes a concrete post, jumps a curb, nearly flies into the air and then lands flat-out in the middle of a *piazza*, right next to a tall obelisk, a stone column with a statue of the Virgin Mary on top.

"We're here!" announces Sister Lisa Renee, turning off the car and smiling with satisfaction.

In a swift set of motions, Sister Lisa Renee opens the door on the driver's side, grabs the dogs, places leashes on them, pulls them out of the back seat, and has them sitting quietly on a curb beside the car.

Sister Philomena, Riley, and Delaney are stunned. Looking out the car windows they see the front of the Basilica Santa Maria Maggiore.

"How in the world did she land us here?" Sister Philomena wonders out loud.

CHAPTER SEVEN

AWAY IN THE MANGER

"**G**ood grief, look at that ceiling!" Riley exclaims, as he and Sister Philomena enter the Basilica Santa Maria Maggiore.

"Isn't it grand?" asks Sister Philomena. "Legend has it that the gold used for the ceiling was brought to Spain by Christopher Columbus on his return from discovering the New World. Queen Isabella of Spain then donated the gold to the Vatican and it was used to gild the ceiling. Here's a history test—when did Columbus discover the New World?"

"That's easy," says Riley. "'In fourteen hundred ninety-two, Columbus sailed the ocean blue.' It's a rhyme we learned in school to remember Columbus' discovery of America. Is this church that old?"

"Yes, and some parts are even older!" answers Sister Philomena. "This church was actually founded in the fourth century. That's only 300 years after Jesus died on the cross. Reportedly an angel appeared to Pope Liberius (who was Pope from 352 until 366) and told him to build a church to honor the Blessed Mother 'on the site where there is snow.' That was in

August, and you know how hot Rome is in the summer. You would never expect to see snow in August! Well, the Pope was guided to this hill and found snow! The first part of the basilica was begun then and along the way, sections and chapels have been added. The ceiling obviously dates back only to the time of Columbus, but that's still a long, long time ago."

"Around the walls are mosaics, pictures made from small colored tiles, that date back to the fifth century. It takes hundreds and hundreds of tiles to make one picture, and they must be fit together like a puzzle. See how well they are preserved. Special craftsmen (also called artisans) from the Vatican Museums care for the art in this basilica. They work hard to keep all the pieces in place, to keep them clean, and to protect them from smog and the layers and layers of dirt that might otherwise harm the art.

"Remember, Riley, the piece of paper contained clues about both the Madonna and the manger, the crib where the infant Jesus was first laid after His birth. The manger relic is below that altar just in front of us. Let's go quietly. Just pretend that we are ordinary tourists."

Sister Philomena and Riley approach the main altar. Narrow marble stairs on both sides descend to an underground chapel. Riley looks down the stairs and into the dimly lit room. He is startled to see an enor-

mous man kneeling before the altar. A chill runs through his body as he realizes the man is made of stone.

"That is a marble sculpture of Pope Pius IX. He was Pope in the 1800s and taught everyone about the Immaculate Conception of Mary," whispers Sister Philomena. "It looks like he's here to keep watch over the manger, doesn't it?"

As Riley's eyes adjust to the low light he can see that the stone Pope is facing a brightly illuminated glass-like object sitting on top of an altar. The object looks like a large glass pot that's about the size of a giant watermelon, is encased in iron bars, and rests on top of a fancy gold box.

"The manger fragments are inside that urn," says Sister Philomena. "The urn looks untouched. Now, I pray that the remaining twenty-four pieces of silver are near it."

Just then an elderly nun with a feather duster appears from behind the altar. The nun gives the urn a few swats with the duster and then begins to straighten the altar cloth beneath the gold box.

Riley spies what looks like another leather pouch, similar to the one they found in the Basilica Saint John Lateran, tucked behind the box.

"She's going for it!" Riley says in a loud whisper, as the elderly nun reaches for the pouch. "Distract her!"

Sister Philomena thinks very quickly and calls to

the nun. "Oh, Sister! Sister! Look here, on the base of this statue of Pope Pius IX. The marble seems to be cracked."

The nun stops dead in her tracks and turns. She half walks, half shuffles over to see what it is that Sister Philomena is pointing towards at the base of the sculpture. The old nun bends down to take a look. Her back is towards Riley so she doesn't see him making a run for the altar.

Standing on his tiptoes, Riley can see the pouch. Unfortunately the pouch is behind the urn, and Riley is not tall enough to reach it. Now what?

Stepping backwards, Riley trips over a kneeler. At first he is embarrassed by the noise it makes, and by his clumsiness. He quickly realizes that the two nuns, still engaged in conversation, are paying no attention to him.

"If I could stand on the kneeler, I could reach the pouch," he thinks to himself.

Quickly he shoves the kneeler over to the altar and steps up onto it. Grabbing the bag, he holds it up to his ear and gives it a shake. The sound of coins clinking together brings a smile to Riley's face. He stuffs the leather pouch in his pants pocket. Quietly he pushes the kneeler back into its place.

Meanwhile, the old nun runs her hand over the base of the statue of Pope Pius IX, with a worrisome look

on her face. She looks up to Sister Philomena and says, *"Non c'é problema. È naturale."* In other words, "It's not a problem. It's natural."

"Ringrazie il Signore," responds Sister Philomena, making the *Sign of the Cross*. "Thank the Lord."

Riley smiles at the old nun as she returns to her cleaning and he rejoins his aunt. "Mission accomplished!" he whispers to his aunt.

"By the way, this isn't stealing, is it?" wonders Riley as he and Sister Philomena start to walk up the stairs. "I'd hate to think of what the penance might be for stealing coins from a church."

"Oh, no," assures Sister Philomena. "We have been sent by the Pope to retrieve stolen property. Our job is to do it quietly and without creating a scandal or scene of any sort."

Hurrying back out into the daylight, they find Sister Lisa Renee, Delaney, and the dogs sitting at the base of the obelisk. Delaney is anxious to tell them something, but Sister Philomena is in a hurry to leave the grounds of the basilica.

"We need to take a break. Sister Lisa Renee, can you drive us to the Piazza Navona where we can get some refreshment?" asks Sister Philomena.

At the Piazza Navona, they pick a quiet table outside one of the many restaurants that surround the oval-shaped *piazza*. "This is a good place to relax," says Sister Philomena, "if it is possible to relax under these circumstances. At the very least, we can have a cool drink and examine the contents of the second pouch. I desperately hope that the rest of the coins are inside.

"Sister Lisa Renee, why don't you take the children and the dogs for a walk around the *piazza* while I wait here for our lemonades?" suggests Sister Philomena.

Riley and Delaney have not been to the Piazza Navona before and can't wait to do some exploring.

"This *piazza* is in the shape of a big oval," explains Sister Lisa Renee. "It was once surrounded by a race track where the ancient Romans held chariot races, but that was ages ago—about 80 A.D., I think. That big fountain in front of us is called the Fountain of the Four Rivers. When it was made, the artist wanted to show the four largest rivers in the known world clashing together. That must be why it's so big. There are two more fountains at each end of the *piazza*. Come, let's take a look!"

The *piazza* is full of activity and seems like a happy place: there are artists selling paintings, people strolling arm-in-arm, a man playing an accordion, children running, mothers pushing baby carriages, and several motionless mimes, dressed up to look like statues. One is dressed as the Statue of Liberty, another as a golden mummy, and a couple, a man and woman, are dressed in white clothes and have white makeup all over their bodies. They look like characters out of a children's storybook.

Riley and Delaney walk up to the mime dressed as the Statue of Liberty. It moves and, to their surprise and delight, bows to them as Sister Lisa Renee tosses a coin into the "donation bucket." "What a weird but fun place is this, the Piazza Navona," thinks Riley.

At the edge of the giant oval, Riley spots a small fountain with water pouring out. He and Delaney drink from the fountain and then begin playing in the water. Riley places his finger over the spout and water shoots high up into the air. The dogs run around madly, trying to catch the falling stream of water.

After a half hour of running around in the hot sun, the dogs seek shelter in the shady area under the table where Sister Philomena is waiting. They stretch, yawn, and then lie down to take a nap.

Delaney and Riley gulp down their lemonades. Exploring the *piazza* in the heat has made them thirsty. The waiter is quick to refill their glasses, and surprises them with a plate of cookies.

Sister Philomena is anxious to share with them what she's figured out about the second note and coins. "As I expected, we retrieved more coins from the Basilica Santa Maria Maggiore—but not as many as I had

hoped. This pouch contained six coins, just like the pouch we retrieved from Basilica Saint John Lateran—and they appear to match those coins. We haven't found all thirty pieces of silver yet, but at least we have twelve of them. Like the first pouch, the Santa Maria Maggiore pouch also contained a note, directing us to another location. The new note uses the word *incarcerare*, which means "to imprison," and also *incatenare*, which means "to chain." It also talks about *San Pietro* or Saint Peter. If I am decoding the puzzle clue properly, we should next go to the Church of Saint Peter in Chains, the Chiesa di San Pietro in Vincoli.

"Finish up your lemonade and let's go!"

As Sister Philomena begins to slip the pouch into the pocket of her habit, Angel, who has been snoozing under the table, opens her eyes and starts to sniff. The dog lifts her head and continues to sniff in the direction of Sister Philomena. Then both Angel and Cielo are up, wagging their tails, and trying to get the pouch from Sister Philomena's pocket.

"What is it with these dogs?" she asks. "These leather pouches seem to really set them off."

"Aunt Philomena, I wanted to tell you something," says Delaney. "When Sister Lisa Renee and I were waiting for you back at the last church, the dogs almost attacked a man. They kept jumping on him and sniffing his pockets like they are doing to you right now. I just thought the man had food in his pocket and they wanted it."

"Good heavens! I wonder if he is the person who is leaving the coins and notes? Do you remember what the man looked like?" Sister Philomena searches the faces of Delaney and Sister Lisa Renee for answers.

Delaney thinks for a moment. "He looked like a lot of other men in Rome. He had black hair and brown eyes and wore a black shirt and grey pants. But this man sounded different. I heard the man talking and his voice was more from here," says Delaney, pointing her finger down her throat.

Sister Philomena stares at Delaney in surprise. "You mean he had an accent?"

"I guess," says Delaney. "His voice wasn't sing-songy like Italians, and not American either. His voice seemed to come up his throat and out his nose."

"That may mean the man's native language is one from the Middle East," says Sister Philomena, impressed with her young niece. "How do you notice these things?"

"I just do," says Delaney. "When the dogs wanted to smell him, I thought I should pay attention."

"Good girl. If you see or hear him again, please let me know. But be careful not to draw attention to your-self. The man may be dangerous."

CHAPTER EIGHT

PETER IN CHAINS

Sister Lisa Renee is behind the wheel again. "I know it's around here somewhere. I just have to find the street. Is this it?" she says, slamming on the brakes. "No, it's on the other side of the Coliseum. Perhaps I should go this way! No, that way." She jabbers to herself while looking for the Church of Saint Peter in Chains. "Riley, can you read that street name? These Rome streets are not well marked and so many of them look the same."

"Hold on!" cautions Riley, as he leans halfway out of the car and struggles to read the small sign on the corner of the Coliseum. "Oh, no, you went by it too fast. Can you drive around again?"

"There it is!" exclaims Sister Lisa Renee in triumph. "Are you kids doing okay?"

The dogs and the children have been taking turns sticking their heads out the car windows. All the stopping and starting and turning and swerving has given them upset stomachs. Delaney figured out from watching the dogs that if she puts her face out the window and breathes in the fresh air, her upset stomach goes away.

"This doesn't even look like a church," Riley observes as he stumbles out of the backseat of the car, clutching his stomach. "It's too long and narrow to be a church. Besides, I don't see a cross on top. All Catholic churches have crosses on top."

"It is a church, I guarantee you," says Sister Philomena. "You'll see. Say, you two aren't sick to your stomachs, are you?"

Afraid that if they open their mouths they will throw up, the kids shake their heads "no."

"Good," says Sister Philomena, relieved. Then she consults her notes. "I have a plan for how we might search this church, and I need your help. I will explain. Inside the church, toward the main altar and just off to the right, is a huge sculpture of Moses that was carved by the artist Michelangelo. You can't miss it—it fills the entire area, floor to ceiling. You can tell it's Moses because he's holding the tablets on which the Ten Commandments are written. I'm thinking the coins maybe hidden somewhere near the sculpture, or they may be near the case that holds the chains of Peter. The note used the words *incarcerare* and *incatenare*, which means to imprison and to chain and that would make me think they should be by the chains.

"What exactly are the chains of Peter—and where are they?" asks a curious Riley.

"The chains of Peter are in a glass case just beneath the main altar. The area is well lighted and we can get fairly close. If I am correct, there are actually two sets of chains joined together," explains Sister Philomena.

"One set is said to be the chains used to imprison the Apostles Peter and Paul in Rome, on or near this very site. The other set dates back to around 40 A.D. when King Herod ruled the Roman Empire. It was a time not long after Jesus was crucified and rose from the dead, but before Peter and Paul came to Rome. Herod was persecuting the Christians and had Peter arrested and put in jail in Jerusalem—you must read about it in your Bibles, in Acts, Chapter 12.

"The story goes that during the night, Peter was bound in chains and was sleeping between two Roman guards. The guards were there to make sure that Peter did not escape. An angel of the Lord appeared to Peter and told him to "Get up quickly." When Peter awoke, he stood up and the chains fell to the ground. The angel led him out of prison to safety. The guards could not figure out how Peter was freed. Upon hearing that Peter escaped, King Herod became very angry and ended up having the guards put to death.

"Wow," says Riley. "I cannot wait to see these chains."

Sister Philomena, Riley, and Delaney go into the church, leaving Sister Lisa Renee in the car with the dogs.

"Did you say that Michelangelo carved this out of marble?" questions Riley as he approaches the sculpture. "I wonder how he ever found a piece of marble that big. Look, Moses is holding the Ten Commandments. This is great!"

"Are those horns on his head?" asks Delaney, pointing to the massive Moses.

"Yes, they are," Sister Philomena responds. "I think Michelangelo was being a little naughty when he made this sculpture. Pope Julius II actually hired Michelangelo to create this piece to be used for the Pope's burial monument. Michelangelo grew frustrated with the job because the Pope kept interrupting and sending Michelangelo off to do other projects. Rather than depicting Moses as having rays of light coming from his head, as it is said he did after he received the tablets from God, Michelangelo gave him horns. Fortunately or unfortunately, Pope Julius II died before the piece was finished. I don't know if he ever got to see the horns or not."

"I don't see a leather pouch," says Riley, after walking and searching from one end of the Moses sculpture to the other. He notices scaffolding that goes up one side of the sculpture, across the top, and down the other, put there so workers can clean the sculpture. "Maybe it's up higher where we can't see it. I can climb up on that scaffolding and look down from above."

"Hold on. Before you do that, let's go look around the chains," says Sister Philomena. "If the pouch is there, you won't have to climb around and draw attention to us."

Sister Philomena takes hold of Delaney's hand to keep her from running off. She can tell by the impish look in the girl's eyes that she is growing restless, and is ready to get into some mischief.

Disappointment creeps into Riley's heart when he doesn't see anything near Peter's chains that resembles a leather pouch or container that would hold the silver coins. "Now what?" he thinks to himself.

"Wait! I think I see something. There, behind the candlestick," Riley whispers to Sister Philomena. "But what I see is a white pouch—it's different from the others. Hmmm, maybe he wanted it to blend in with the altar and not be so noticeable.

"Aunt Philomena, there are so many people in here, I don't think we can take the pouch without being noticed. Besides, that guard over there has been watching us closely. I think he suspects something's up," continues Riley in a deep whisper.

"We'll have to create a distraction," says Sister Philomena. She thinks about it for a second. As Delaney begins to tug at her sleeve impatiently, Sister Philomena gets an idea.

"Riley, we'll create a scene to distract the guard. As soon as you see the guard look away from the altar of the chains, you run up there and grab the pouch," instructs Sister Philomena. "Ready?" Again Riley wonders if stealing from a church is wrong—but then he remembers that this is an official investigation, begun at the request of the Pope, so it must be okay.

Then Sister Philomena gives Delaney an assignment. "Go run in circles in the middle of the church—
go around three times, singing something really loud.
After the third time, run to the statue of Moses and
start climbing on the scaffolding. But be careful not to
fall! When I call you, come right down and over to
me."

Sister Philomena lets go of Delaney's hand. As she
suspected, Delaney is more than ready to do her part.
She charges ahead, running in circles and singing at
the top of her lungs, then heads for the scaffolding and
starts to climb.

"Delaney, you get down from there!" shouts Sister
Philomena. "Right now! Do you hear me?"

The distraction has worked. The guard and almost
everyone else in the church has turned to watch the
little girl who is now halfway up the scaffolding—and
the nun who is trying to make her come back down.
Some of the tourists laugh at the sight of a nun trying
to discipline such an energetic little girl.

When no one is looking, Riley quickly reaches up
behind the candlestick and grabs the pouch. The size
and weight of this pouch seem to match that of the
other pouches. He is certain this is it.

Turning around, Riley can see Sister Philomena
helping Delaney climb down the scaffolding. What a
team the three of them make!

77

"Delaney, let's go over to the altar and say a prayer," says Sister Philomena, taking the girl by the hand, giving her a wink, and whispering, "Good job!"

Delaney beams from ear to ear.

Sister Philomena and Delaney walk toward Riley and the glass case with the chains. She gives him the "eye" and he gives her a big "thumbs-up."

As they kneel to pray, they see the guard and tourists have gone back to their own business. No one is aware of what just happened.

Riley slides the pouch to Sister Philomena, who peeks inside and says, "Yes, it's there!" But Sister Philomena's joy turns to disappointment and frustration when she sees only six coins, and yet another note! "When will this end?" she wonders.

CHAPTER NINE

THE HOLY STEPS

Climbing back into the little red car, Sister Philomena has to fight off the dogs as she tries to read the note in the pouch. Delaney grabs one dog and Riley grabs the other, to keep them away from their aunt.

Sister Lisa Renee revs the engine of the little red car. Looking and sounding like a racecar driver ready for takeoff, "Where to, next?" she asks.

"Hold on while I try to decipher this note." Sister Philomena is getting weary, but the excitement of the search keeps her going. After a few minutes of reading and studying the note, she thinks she has figured it out. "I believe we are to go to the Scala Santa next. It's not far from here, is it?" She looks around to figure out where in Rome they are now.

"It's back there, next to the Basilica Saint John Lateran," says Sister Lisa Renee. Without warning, she makes a big U-turn in the middle of traffic. Several drivers slam on their brakes to avoid hitting the little red car, while others swerve, just missing it. But Sister Lisa

Renee just smiles and waves to the other drivers who are now shouting and angrily waving their fists at her.

It's clear that Sister Philomena is used to Sister Lisa Renee's driving. Although her body dips and rolls in the front seat while Sister Lisa Renee zips through traffic, she too ignores the insults of the other drivers. Looking at her notes, all she says is, "Hurry. It's getting late. We now have eighteen of the thirty coins. How much further do we need to go?"

Arriving in front of the Scala Santa, Riley reads the words chiseled in the stone over the doorway.

"*Sanctus*—doesn't that mean 'holy' in Latin? I've heard that word used often, like in the *sanctus, sanctus, sanctus,* or 'holy, holy, holy' during Mass. But what does *scala* mean?" asks Riley.

"It means steps," explains Sister Philomena. "The *Scala Santa* in Italian, or *Scala Sancta* in Latin, or Holy Steps in English, are the steps that were in front of Pontius Pilate's residence in Jerusalem. You know how we say, 'Jesus suffered under Pontius Pilate?' Well, these are the very steps Jesus walked on the day He was tortured, suffered, and was crucified."

"How can that be? Wasn't Pontius Pilate's house in Jerusalem? How did they get here?" asks a bewildered Riley.

"Oh, the steps were in Jerusalem, but they were

moved here in the fourth century. Saint Helen rescued them from Jerusalem in the year 328 and brought them here to Rome for safekeeping.

"Hundreds of pilgrims ascend these steps on their knees each day to recall Jesus' Way of the Cross. God grants special grace to the pilgrims who climb the steps, if they are in the right frame of mind. The steps are made of stone, but have been covered with wood to preserve them. Every so often you find little glassed-in windows in the wood. You can look through the windows and see dried blood—it's Jesus' blood!

"If we want to go to the top, we have to walk up the steps on our knees, too. Along the way we shall meditate on The Way of the Cross. Are you up to it?"

"I wouldn't miss it," says Riley. The thought of walking, or actually kneeling, in the footsteps of Jesus, and seeing actual drops of His blood, nearly blows his mind. Riley wonders, "How come I am so lucky to be here and to get to do this? And to think I thought this was going to be a boring summer. Whew!"

"Can Delaney come too? I don't think she knows about The Way of the Cross, but she could use the grace. It's like the Stations of the Cross isn't it?"

"I do too know!" retorts Delaney. "I did the Stations of the Cross last year during Lent with my teacher. Only we did them outside in a garden."

Sister Philomena is amazed at how well the children

remember things from their religious education classes in the United States. Their teachers are to be congratulated.

"That's wonderful, Delaney. But we have to walk up these steps on our knees, and in absolute silence," warns Sister Philomena. She quietly prays that the little girl behaves in this sacred place.

Sister Philomena, Riley, and Delaney ascend the twenty-eight steps of the Scala Santa on their knees, as do the other people visiting the holy site today. Although it has been a long day and they feel tired and discouraged, they begin. By the time they reach the top of the stairs, they feel refreshed. The Lord has blessed them.

"This is the main chapel in front of us," explains Sister Philomena as they stand at the top of the stairs. In addition, there are three other chapels around to the right and in back of this chapel. Let's go look for our silver coins," encourages Sister Philomena.

There is nothing evident in the main chapel. Nothing is found in the other chapels either.

"Uh oh, was this a false lead? Or did I misinterpret the clue?" wonders Sister Philomena.

She's ready to search the area one more time when a nun emerges from the small gift shop near the top of the stairs.

"Are you Sister Philomena?" the nun asks.

"Why, yes I am. Do you know me?"

"Not really," replies the nun, "but a gentleman asked me to give you this package. He said I could identify you because you probably would have two children with you—two American children."

"Grazie," says Sister Philomena.

As she takes the package, a shiver runs down her spine. "Has the puzzler been watching us all day? Who is the puzzler? Where is he? What does he look like?" she wonders to herself.

"Sister, can you tell me anything about the man who left this box?" Sister Philomena asks in an urgent voice.

"He was here maybe an hour or two ago," replies the nun. "I had a feeling he was not from Rome. Perhaps he is an Israeli or from somewhere else in the Middle East."

"I'm scared," says Riley, looking around. "He's been watching us."

"Don't be afraid," his aunt reassures him. "Trust in the Lord and He will protect us. After all, we are doing His business. Now, I think we should go back to Father Allen's office in the Vatican to open this package and rest a bit. In his office we'll be able to spread out all of the clues we've gathered so far."

CHAPTER TEN

SOLVING THE PUZZLE

"**I**'m not sure you can bring those dogs inside," Sister Philomena tells Sister Lisa Renee. Sister Lisa Renee is attempting to park the little red car in a dark corner of the interior of the Vatican, near the entrance to the Sistine Chapel and Father Allen's office, but out of view from the Holy Father's window.

"The dogs will be fine," assures Sister Lisa Renee. "I can keep them quiet and out of people's way. Besides, it's after business hours and there won't be many people around."

The two nuns, two kids, and two dogs get out of the car. The Swiss Guard on duty this evening has met Sister Philomena before and knows that she works directly for the Pope. He assumes that it's okay to allow her and her companions, including the dogs, into the building. He opens the door for them to enter.

In the eerie quiet of late afternoon, the group ascends the wide marble staircase, walks down the corridor with walls that are covered in art, passes through an arched doorway, and enters Father Allen's office.

Flipping on the lights, Sister Philomena spies a note from Father Allen. The note says that she is welcome to use his office this evening. However, some Patrons from the U.S. are visiting and he and his assistants, Giovanna and Sara, may be in and out of the office from time to time.

Sister Philomena drops her black valise onto Father Allen's desk and then empties the contents of her pockets: two brown leather pouches, one white leather pouch, and a box, each containing six silver coins and a handwritten note.

The dogs jump up on their hind legs and begin sniffing around the desk. Soon they tire of trying to get anything off the desk and begin investigating the rest of the room, sniffing every nook and cranny. Convinced that there is nothing else very interesting to smell, both dogs jump up onto the plush couch in Father Allen's office—the couch that is generally reserved for very important visitors. Sister Philomena is about to protest, then stops, deciding that it is probably a waste of energy to try to keep the dogs off the furniture. At least if they are sleeping they will be quiet.

As Delaney climbs up to snuggle with the two dogs, Sister Philomena digs more deeply into the mystery of the thirty pieces of silver. She moves to the wall beside the desk and presses the edges of two panels of the rich dark wood that line Father Allen's office. The wall panels pop open to display a bulletin board on one side and a chalkboard on the other.

She pulls a map of Rome from her valise and pins it to the bulletin board. Next, she removes the notes from the pouches and the box and carefully thumb-tacks them next to the map of Rome, placing them in the order in which they were discovered. Finally, she uses pushpins to mark the locations on the map where the coins were found:

1. *San Giovanni in Laterano/Saint John Lateran*
2. *Santa Maria Maggiore*
3. *San Pietro in Vincoli/Saint Peter in Chains*
4. *Scala Santa/Holy Steps*

On the chalkboard, Sister Philomena begins to list the questions that must be answered to solve the puzzle:

1. *What do these places have in common?*
2. *Is there a pattern?*
3. *Is the handwriting always the same? Memo: Get a handwriting analysis.*
4. *Is the paper used always the same? Memo: Get a paper analysis.*

5. What is the scent or smell that attracts the dogs?
6.

Just as she is about to write down another question, Sister Philomena remembers that she has not yet read the note from the Scala Santa. "I must be more tired than I thought. How could I forget to read the note?"

Stopping everything, Sister Philomena goes to the fourth note pinned on the bulletin board and reads.

"I don't believe this!" she exclaims.

"What does it say?" questions Riley. He too is tired, but is also extremely curious and hoping to be able to solve this puzzle.

"I believe the answer is very close to us, and I fear that the perpetrator has been watching us all along. The note indicates that the answer lies in the Sistine Chapel."

"What!?" exclaims a now very-much-awake Riley.

Quietly so as not to disturb the others, Sister Philomena tiptoes to a far corner of the office and gently taps on one of the wood panels. Suddenly the panel rolls open to reveal a dimly lit passageway. Riley's eyes get as big as saucers and he is speechless as his aunt motions for him to follow her.

"I doubt that Father Allen even knows this passageway exists," whispers Sister Philomena. The passage-

way, like the office, is lined with rich, dark, wood paneling. Curiously, it seems to come to a dead end. Sister Philomena stands in front of the dead-end wall and taps its center. The wall begins to rotate, revealing a room about the size of a schoolroom, but with artwork on the walls and ceiling. On the other side of the room is a double door. Riley is amazed when his aunt walks over and casually opens it. Surprise, surprise—this is a secret entrance into the Sistine Chapel.

Rays of late afternoon sun stream through the windows high up on the chapel's walls. Although it is now hard to see the ceiling of the chapel because of the sun's rays, the walls are clearly visible.

It is dead quiet, but the silence doesn't last long.

"Stop! Sit!! Stay!! Come, Angel! Come, Cielo!! No, don't go there!!!" shouts the panic-stricken Sister Lisa Renee, her voice echoing off of the walls inside what was a 'secret' passageway. The dogs come racing into the Sistine Chapel, followed close behind by Sister Lisa Renee and Delaney.

"We forgot to close the doors!" cries Riley. When he and Sister Philomena left the office, Delaney was sound asleep, and Sister Lisa Renee was nodding off in the big chair. They didn't even think to close the panels to the passageway.

"Dear God, forgive us for letting these animals

loose in your sacred chapel," Sister Philomena prays out loud. "*O, Dio Mio!* Perhaps Your love of animals, and my love of You, together are enough to receive your forgiveness for this recklessness. I need Your help, dear Lord. Please, I pray."

The dogs race through the chapel with their noses to the ground. It looks as if they are tracking a rabbit: running forward then switching back, around and around, back and forth they go. Finally they stop and sit side by side with their tails wagging and their faces turned up, looking at the wall.

Sister Lisa Renee rushes up and attaches leashes to their collars. She tries to lead them away from the wall, tugging on their leashes, but they resist and begin to howl loudly. "Oh, no!" Sister Lisa Renee cries, as she grabs hold of Angel and places a hand over her muzzle in an attempt to stifle the howling. Delaney does the same with Cielo. Then they pick the dogs up and carry them back to Father Allen's office, closing the doors and panels behind them.

Silence having been restored in the Sistine Chapel, Sister Philomena and Riley study the note from the Scala Santa for clues.

"Look at this," suggests Sister Philomena. "It looks like three words are coming out from the letter 'A' in the middle of the page. It's sort of a pinwheel shape.

You can see better than I can—what do you make them out to be?"

Riley struggles to read the note in the dim light, but can make out letters and spells them out for Sister Philomena. "It looks like g-o-n-y, r-r-e-s-t, and t-o-n-e-m-e-n-t."

"Hmmm," mutters Sister Philomena. "Put the 'A' in front of each of them and you have the words *agony*, *arrest*, and *atonement*. Now where in the Sistine Chapel do we find agony, arrest, and atonement?"

She and Riley begin to search the images on the walls and ceiling of the Sistine Chapel trying to find a scene or panel that would represent AGONY, ARREST, and ATONEMENT.

Beginning on the left side, they study the frescos representing events in the life of Moses. Nothing pops out. Then they direct their attention to the Last Judgment, the scene painted on the big wall behind the altar. Surely the Last Judgment portrays the AGONY of the souls being sent to Hell. But ARREST and ATONEMENT—these are not the messages of the Last Judgment. "Judgment is judgment!" comments Sister Philomena. "Time for ATONEMENT is past!"

Slowly they turn to the right side of the chapel and begin studying its frescos. This side contains the pictures representing events in the life of Jesus Christ.

"That's it!" shouts Sister Philomena. "There at the

end, the picture of the Last Supper. This is the same wall where the dogs got so excited. This clue has led us to the Last Supper!"

"I don't get it," a puzzled Riley says. "What do AGONY, ARREST, and ATONEMENT have to do with the Last Supper?"

"Look at the pictures the artist has painted in the windows above the Last Supper. See, there are pictures inside the picture. Those small pictures in the big picture of the Last Supper tell the story of the Passion of Christ.

"See, the first picture or window shows Jesus with Peter, James, and John praying in the garden—that's the AGONY in the Garden.

"The second picture is of the ARREST of Jesus. That's Judas giving Jesus a kiss on the cheek—the kiss that told the Roman soldiers that this was Jesus. That's when Judas received the thirty pieces of silver. Oh, my goodness, we are onto something here!

"The third picture or window shows Jesus crucified."

"But I don't understand where ATONEMENT comes in," says Riley. "Jesus didn't sin! Doesn't ATONEMENT mean to give up sin or sacrifice to be reconciled with God—or something like that?"

"Oh, Riley! It does. It does." Sister Philomena is almost too excited to speak. "Look, look, look! Jesus

was crucified between two other men, see them in the picture. The one on the right is the bad thief. The one on the left, which is Jesus' right, is called the good thief.

"Just before he died, the good thief became AT ONE, or ATONED or reconciled, with God through Jesus' sacrifice. I love this story so much, I have memorized the Scripture, from Luke, Chapter 23:

. . . *Now two others, both criminals, were led away with him to be executed. When they came to the place called the Skull, they crucified him and the criminals there, one on his right, the other on his left.*

. . . *Now one of the criminals hanging there reviled Jesus, saying, "Are you not the Messiah? Save yourself and us."*

That would be the bad thief.

. . . *The other, however, rebuking him, said in reply, "Have you no fear of God, for you are subject to the same condemnation? And indeed, we have been condemned justly, for the sentence we received corresponds to our crimes, but this man has done nothing criminal." Then he said, "Jesus, remember me when you come into your kingdom." He replied to him, "Amen, I say to you, today you will be with me in Paradise."*

Sister Philomena and Riley stand for a long while, studying the picture. "I think I understand," says Riley. "But how does it solve the puzzle?"

"Well, I don't have the answer. However, I feel we are close, very close," says Sister Philomena. "Let's pray on it. We are in one of the most holy places on earth, the Sistine Chapel, where Popes are elected, where the Holy Father holds special services, where we can study the life of Moses, the life of Jesus, the Old and New Testaments. We need to pray."

Holding hands, Sister Philomena and Riley pray the *Our Father,* the *Hail Mary,* and the *Glory Be to the Father.* Then they turn to go back to Father Allen's office.

"Wait, what's that under the bench?" asks Riley, pointing to a small parcel, which just happens to be under the picture of the Last Supper, and at the same spot where the dogs made such a fuss.

Riley picks up the package and hands it to Sister Philomena. It's lighter than the other packages.

CHAPTER ELEVEN

THE TRUE CROSS

"**G**iovanna brought us food," blurts out Delaney with her mouth full as Sister Philomena and Riley return to Father Allen's office. "She says it's leftovers from the Patrons' dinner. Look at their leftovers!"

A delightful looking buffet is set up on Father Allen's work table. There is an *antipasto* platter with pickled fish, mushrooms, onions, sliced tomatoes, and little balls of fresh mozzarella cheese. Another platter has risotto, a creamy Italian rice dish prepared with Parmesan cheese and sliced mushrooms. Next to the risotto is a platter of thinly sliced beef surrounded by stuffed tomatoes and green beans. Finally, there is a plate with four slices of tiramisu, a dessert whose name means "pick-me-up," made with layers of cake and whipped cream and topped with cocoa.

"The caterer just gave me these, too," says a jubilant Giovanna, rushing back into the office. She is carrying two bone-shaped objects. "Dog treats!"

"*Grazie*! My dogs will love you!" says Sister Lisa Renee.

Giovanna explains to an amazed Sister Philomena that all of this food was left over from a lunch catered in the Museums and hosted by His Eminence Cardinal Kelly from America. The dinner is for the Patrons of the Arts in the Vatican Museums who are visiting Rome and the Vatican this week. When they have an opportunity to visit the Museums, the Patrons are always treated with the highest respect. The dinner is a way to say "thank you" for their generosity. Giovanna explained that the caterers prepared much more food than the Patrons could eat. "Rather than throw it out, Father Allen suggested that perhaps you and your companions would enjoy it."

"It sure looks a lot better than convent food," jokes Riley.

"Thank you, Giovanna. God bless you, child. We have been so intent on our assignment today that we completely forgot to eat."

As they eat, Riley stares at the notes pinned to the bulletin board. He notices that each note has a peculiar style of lettering. And each note has at least one large letter.

"Aunt Philomena, does d-m-i-s-a spell anything? Or maybe d-m-i-s-s-a?"

"No, not that I am aware of. Why do you ask?" questions Sister Philomena.

"When you look at the notes from this far away you can see that each one has a big letter. One letter is capitalized and is much larger than any of the others." Riley goes to the bulletin board to point out what he sees.

"The D from the word *Decapitate* on the note for Saint John Lateran,

"The M on the word *Madonna* on the note for Santa Maria Maggiore,

"I from *Incatenare* on the note from San Pietro in Vincoli,

"S or SS from the Scala Santa note,

"and a big A on the note that sent us to the Sistine Chapel. The 'A' is in the middle of the three words, agony, arrest, and atonement, but it is as big as the letters on the other notes."

"DMISSA…" Sister Philomena sounds out the letters. "Or, if you jumble the letters, it could be MISSDA."

"Does D-I-S-M-A-S spell anything?" questions Riley.

Sister Philomena traces the letters on the palm of her hand. "It's the good thief!" Her eyes brighten as she remembers.

"Who?" Sister Lisa Renee, Delaney, and Riley ask all at once. Delaney looks around to see if there is a thief in the room.

"I have a feeling that the answer to this entire puzzle has something to do with the good thief, the one from the crucifixion—you know, the thief from the picture in the Sistine Chapel," says Sister Philomena. "His name was Dismas."

"I don't get it? Is the puzzler saying he's a good thief?" asks Riley.

Sister Philomena ponders Riley's question for a few moments. "Got it!" she cries, snapping her fingers. "Let's go. Sister Lisa Renee, get the keys. Come along, children, we have one more stop yet to make this evening."

"But we haven't eaten dessert," protests Delaney, "and tiramisu is one of my favorites!"

"I know. Just wrap it up and you can take it with you to eat in the car," says Sister Philomena without thinking.

They all pile back into the little red car. Sister Lisa Renee turns on the ignition and the windshield wipers scrape the dry glass with an irritating bumping sound.

"Mi dispiace," cries Sister Lisa Renee. She flips every lever and twists every knob on the dashboard—and the radio blares, water spurts from the washer onto the windshield, the horn beeps, the dogs begin to bark, and the Swiss Guard start running towards the car. Suddenly the headlights pop on. "Finally!" she sings. *"Ciao,"* she waves to the Swiss Guards. "Where to?"

she asks, turning to Sister Philomena, who is smiling at her in amusement.

"Drive back to Basilica Saint John Lateran, and then drive directly south from the basilica to the end of the road," instructs Sister Philomena. We need to get to the Basilica Santa Croce in Gerusalemme as fast as possible. But safely," she adds quickly.

Sister Philomena turns around when she hears giggling and licking sounds coming from the backseat. "What's going on back there? Oh, dear! Are you all right? I'm sorry, I should have known better."

Delaney has tiramisu smeared all over her hands and face and the dogs are frantically trying to lick it off. "It tickles," cries Delaney as she tries to smear the tiramisu on the faces of the dogs. Before Sister Lisa Renee can stop the car so the mess can be cleaned up, the dogs have licked away every crumb and smudge of the sweet, creamy dessert.

The sun is setting by the time they arrive at the Basilica Santa Croce in Gerusalemme. The basilica looms large over the *piazza* that fills in the area between the basilica and the road. Not seeing a proper parking space, Sister Lisa Renee decides to create her own by driving the little red car onto the pedestrian area of the *piazza* and turning off the engine. Sister Philomena closes her eyes, shakes her head, and wordlessly takes Riley with her into the basilica.

The basilica is big, but not as big as Saint Peter's or Saint John Lateran's.

"Wait, what's that?" asks Riley, pointing to the main altar.

On the dome over the altar is a stunning mosaic of Jesus sitting on a throne, behind which is a beautiful blue starry sky. Jesus is giving a blessing. Beneath Him and encircling the dome are pictures depicting the history of the True Cross. Sister Philomena explains again that Saint Helen was responsible for bringing many relics of Jesus' Passion to Rome, including the Holy Steps they climbed on their knees earlier today. The pictures he is looking at tell the story of how the True Cross was rescued and brought to Rome.

"This way," cautions Sister Philomena. "I am hoping our 'good thief' is hiding in the Sanctuary of the Cross."

Taking Riley by the hand, Sister Philomena leads him up a magnificent marble stairway and down a hallway on the left side of the basilica. Riley can feel in his bones that they are entering a special place. Along the hallway walls are symbols of the Way of the Cross. "It makes sense," Riley thinks to himself, "seeing as this is the church of the Holy Cross."

It is very quiet. Riley's heart is racing as he faces a

large, brightly illuminated glass case. Candles burn on each side of the case and there is a simple, small altar in front.

"What are those?" he asks, taking a closer look at the contents of the case.

"Those are the relics of the Passion of our Lord, Jesus Christ," explains Sister Philomena.

She glances around and sees that there is nowhere in this room for the puzzler to hide. "Perhaps I misinterpreted the clue," she thinks, feeling extremely disappointed. But, rather than waste this trip, she can at least show her nephew these most precious relics.

"That cross in the center contains fragments from the True Cross—the one on which Jesus was crucified.

"In the reliquary below it, to the left, is one of the nails from the crucifixion. Look, it appears to be slightly bent. Beside the nail is the *Titulus Crucis*. That's the wooden tablet stating the charges that Pontius Pilate brought against Christ—you remember, how He was 'King of the Jews.'

"There on the top shelf, those two needle-like objects—they are thorns from the crown of thorns."

"What's in that one?" Riley asks, pointing to the reliquary on the upper left.

"Are you ready for this?" asks Sister Philomena, preparing Riley for a great surprise. "That is believed to be the finger of Saint Thomas the Apostle. The very

finger he placed in the side of Jesus after His resurrection."

"Wow! No way!" Riley is too amazed to say anything else.

"Why is that old piece of wood inside the case?" Riley asks, as he regains his composure.

"Oh, that is what made me think to come here," says Sister Philomena. "That is the bar of the cross on which the good thief, our Dismas, hung."

"No way!" Riley gasps again. "How can all this be here—just be here? And we can get so close to it!"

"Say a prayer of thanksgiving for Saint Helen and for all the souls that risked their lives to save these precious relics."

CHAPTER TWELVE

THE CURSE

Riley hears the howl of hounds off in the distance. It must be the beagles. Then Sister Philomena hears it too. She frowns and looks at Riley.

The howling grows louder and louder, sounding more like crying yelps.

They hear voices—faint at first, then louder. The voices sound like those of people in distress. Listening more intently, they recognize the voices of Sister Lisa Renee and Delaney!

Something terrible must be happening. Without a word, Sister Philomena and Riley turn away from the relics and run back down the stairs.

As they reach the base of the main altar, they hear a door crash open. A flash of light comes from the direction of the front door, and then disappears. Next comes the sound of footsteps, like somebody running into the basilica and towards them. It's too dark to see who it is or where the person went, but the sounds of heavy breathing and running footsteps are unmistakable.

Riley strains to hear and see. His heart is beating so

loudly in his ears that it drowns out all other sounds. Then he sees, or thinks he sees, a dark figure racing along the wall on the opposite side of the basilica.

Suddenly the double doors at the front of the basilica burst open and the long rays of the late afternoon sunshine stream in. In the streaks of light, Riley watches the running figure disappear into a passageway near the altar.

The sound of dogs howling and yelping suddenly fills the basilica. Riley turns in time to see Angel and Cielo running through the double doors and into the church. Sister Lisa Renee and Delaney are holding onto the dogs' leashes and are being dragged into the church behind the barking dogs. But the dogs are too strong for them, and pull the leashes out of their hands. The dogs charge around the basilica with their noses to the ground, stopping periodically to give a yelp and a howl, just like they did in the Sistine Chapel. Clearly they are on the scent of something.

The dogs run into the passageway, the same passageway where Riley saw the running figure disappear.

"Go that way! Follow the dogs!" shouts Riley.

Sister Philomena and Riley are the first to reach the passageway, with Sister Lisa Renee and Delaney just steps behind.

"It's the man from the other place. The place where we waited in front of the church for you—the church with the manger," says Delaney. "The dogs kept smelling and pestering that man! Then we saw him standing outside this church too! The dogs started barking and wanting to get to him. When the man saw us, he ran in here!"

"Wait a minute!" Sister Philomena stops her three companions from chasing after the dogs who have just run into the passageway. "This passageway leads down one level to the Chapel of Saint Helen. There is a second passageway into the chapel on the other side of the altar. Let's split up.

"You two enter from this side," Sister Philomena says to Sister Lisa Renee and Riley. "Delaney, you come with me and we'll enter from the other side. We'll trap the puzzler in the middle. When I wave my hand, we enter."

Barking and growling sounds rumble up from below. Is it possible the dogs have reached the puzzler?

On signal, the nuns and children enter the opposing passageways and descend to the Chapel of Saint Helen. The passageways are dark, but burning votive candles provide just enough light to see inside the chapel.

"There he is!" shrieks Delaney.

"They caught him!" cheers Riley.

"Please, call off the dogs," pleads the man. He has dark hair and is wearing a black shirt and grey pants, matching the description that Delaney gave earlier. "Please, let me explain."

"*Buono...* Good dog, Angel. Good dog, Cielo. Come!" Sister Lisa Renee reaches into her pocket and pulls out the two treats that Giovanna gave her earlier.

The dogs reluctantly turn away from the man, but eagerly take the treats and lie down to chew on them.

The man is cowering in what looks like a sandbox. The sandbox smells old and sour—a smell that perhaps only dogs would find appealing. In the man's fingers are two slightly sandy pieces of silver. It looks like he has just dug the coins out of the sand and is preparing to put them in a leather pouch.

"What stinks?" asks Delaney, holding her nose.

"Is that what I think it is?" Sister Philomena inquires, pointing to the sand in the sandbox.

"I believe so," says the man. "This is the sand brought to Rome from Jerusalem, from Calvary, the place where Jesus was crucified. I know this to be true. I also knew it would be a good place for me to hide my coins since not many people come down to this chapel these days. But, I didn't expect it to smell this way. Perhaps over the years too many tourists have placed items in the sand and caused it to stink."

"But that sand is sacred," complains Sister Philomena. "Why are you here?"

"Please! Please! Let me explain." The man sounds desperate.

"My name is Dismay. I am a Christian of Jewish decent. I have come here from Jerusalem. Months ago, I sent these coins to the Holy Father," he says, holding up the coins he has just dug from the sandbox.

"I asked that they be authenticated as the coins, the thirty pieces of silver, paid to Judas to betray Christ. But I was nearly certain that these were the very same coins, the thirty pieces of silver. History has convinced me of this.

"My main reason for sending the coins here was to rid my family of the evil that has followed it since they took possession of the coins during the time of Christ. I hoped that the Holy Father would bless the coins and the curse would go away, and after that, the evil one would finally leave us alone."

"You are not making sense," Sister Philomena says, with a perplexed look on her face.

"Let me explain further," Dismay pleads.

"You see, my family is descended from the man named Dismas—the so-called 'good thief.' Our family has possessed these coins for nearly 2000 years, passing them from generation to generation. Each and every generation has experienced evil and tragedy, and I believe it is because of these coins.

"Before Jesus and my ancestor Dismas were cruci-fied, Judas gave the thirty pieces of silver back to the Pharisees. This is confirmed in the Bible as well as by legends passed down by my family."

Riley looks at Sister Philomena in near disbelief. He remembers what she told him in the Sistine Chapel about the good thief, Dismas. Now, this guy says he is related to the good thief.

"Judas was evil and then went off and hung him-self—that was an evil act," the puzzler, Dismay, con-tinues. "So, I believe that from the very beginning that whoever had possession of these coins would be cursed—or at the least be prone to evil ways.

"When Judas returned the coins to the Pharisees, these Jewish men realized that they could not keep the coins. The coins were used to send someone to his death and therefore were considered blood money and thus were unclean. The Jewish law forbid taking unclean items into the Temple. Instead, the Pharisees used the thirty pieces of silver to purchase land to be used as a burial place for foreigners, the poor, and homeless. The land was bought from a potter and the burial place became known as the Potter's Field. I am told that my ancestor, Dismas, was buried in this very

field following his death on the cross.

"I am also told that Dismas' brothers and children were thieves too. While Dismas was being buried, his very own brother and one of his sons sneaked into the potter's house and stole the thirty pieces of silver.

"From that day onward, the family has been plagued by misfortune and misdeeds. Many became thieves, some were murderers, most of them were liars and cheaters—they were just bad people. Even the children were ornery, mean bullies, and gang leaders.

"When I looked back over our family history, all I could see was evil, and the pattern followed the possession of these coins. It was tragic.

"I realized that I had an obligation to change the course of this behavior. Besides becoming a good and holy Christian myself, I realized I needed to rid my family of these coins and the evil that follows them.

"One day I got this bright idea. I thought perhaps if the coins were in the Pope's possession, the evil would go away. The more I studied, the more I became convinced that the Pope's blessing would rid these coins of the devil's curse.

"But the coins never got to the Pope. They were given first to the Vatican Museums' staff to be authenticated. For whatever reason, the coins were not processed and sat for a long time. As weeks went by, I became fearful that the good people who accidentally came in contact with the coins would also encounter evil. The fear became so great inside me that I just had to do something.

"Recently I was walking around Rome, visiting lots of churches and basilicas, and the idea came to me: I should steal back the coins and leave them in holy places in Rome. My hope was that if I were to leave the coins in some of these very holy places, the blessings given by the priests during Masses and the prayers of pilgrims would counteract the evil. So that's what I did, I left the coins all over Rome.

"But why the notes, why not just leave the coins and be done with it?" asks Sister Philomena.

"Because I think the Pope should have the coins," replies Dismay. "I trust that he will know if they should be kept or destroyed. I wanted the evil to go away but not the artifacts themselves. That is why I left the notes—so that they could be found and restored to the Church."

Sister Philomena stares at Dismay for a long time. She is not sure she can believe his story.

"Whew, this place does stink," she finally announces. "Let's get out of here. I think we should take you back to meet the director of the Vatican

Museums and Capitano Leo of the Swiss Guard. They can determine the authenticity of your story and decide if we need to press charges.

"Have you been following us around Rome all day?" Sister Philomena asks the man.

"Yes. I hired a driver," says Dismay. "We went to the places where I had left the coins and added the notes. Then we circled around to watch you as you arrived, searched the premises, and left for the next site. I was honestly afraid for you and the children, afraid that the evil that follows the coins would harm you.

"My driver and I have been impressed with Sister Lisa Renee's miraculous avoidance of mishap this entire day. She drives like no one I have ever seen. Perhaps the fact that she did not have a terrible accident all day proves that the coins have lost their evil curse. The blessings of the holy places must have worked."

"Perhaps," cautions Sister Philomena. "But consider that coins themselves have no evil power. The evil power you witnessed is actually the work of the devil, using the coins as a tool to lure people, like your family, into evil ways. However, you have found the courage to seek God's help in breaking this cycle of behavior. It is you, Dismay, who is blessed.

"Please allow me to introduce you to our skillful driver," says Sister Philomena as they exit the basilica and walk towards the little red car. "Being a courageous and blessed man, you surely won't mind riding back to the Vatican with Sister Lisa Renee. You will no doubt be convinced that the curse is gone once we arrive safely at the Vatican."

Sister Lisa Renee blushes and tries to exit the car, but her habit gets tangled in the parking brake, causing it to release accidentally. The car rolls forward a few feet and crashes into a no parking sign before coming to a stop.

Hesitantly, Dismay hands the remaining coins to Sister Philomena, sighs deeply, and stoops to enter the car's tiny back seat. The dogs, following his scent, jump in on top of Dismay, and then Riley and Delaney squeeze in on either side.

The two nuns hop in the front seats. Sister Lisa Renee cranks the engine, pops the clutch, and drives over the no parking sign. Mission accomplished!

=== THE END ===

Italian Words and Phrases Learned on This Adventure

*Le parole e le frasi italiane
che abbiamo imparato
in questa avventura*

$\mathbb{T}$raveling to foreign places and meeting people from other countries is always exciting. Even if you travel only in your thoughts while reading about foreign places and people, the experience is still very exciting. Learning to communicate with people from other countries makes a trip that much more fun. Here are some words and phrases that Riley and Delaney would have learned in this adventure, *Curse of the Coins*.

Parole italiane in questo libro	Italian Words in This Book (English translation!)
vada prego	please go *or* go, I pray
decapitare	to decapitate, to behead
sacchetto	bag
d'argento	(of) silver
mamma mia	good gracious!
monete	coins
venite qui	come here
sedete	sit
andiamo	let's go
casa grande	big house
rubato	stolen

salvato	saved
incarcerare	to imprison
incatenare	to chain
ringrazie il Signore	thank the Lord
non c'è problema	it's not a problem
scala	step *or* stair
santa (Italian)	
sanctus (Latin)	holy
grazie	thank you

Indicazioni Direzionale / Directions

senso unico / one way

sosta vietata / no parking

deviazione / detour

spingere / push

tirare / pull

nord / north

sud / south

est / east

ovest / west

su / up

giu / down

questa strada / this road *or* street

sopra / above

sotto / beneath

dietro / in back of

davanti / in front of

vicino / near

127

Luoghi in città / Places in the city

l'agenzia / the agency
il bar / the bar (really a coffee shop in Italy)
il centro / the center or downtown
la farmacia / the pharmacy
il mercato / the market
il museo / the museum
la banca / the bank
l'ospedale / the hospital
la piazza / the plaza or square
il ristorante / the restaurant
lo stadio / the stadium
la stazione / the station
il supermercato / the supermarket
il teatro / the theater

Parti dell'automobile / Parts of the car

i fari / the headlights
il cofano / the hood
la parabrezza / the windshield
il tergicristallo / the windshield wiper
il finestrino / the window
la portiera / the door
la maniglia / the door handle
la radio / the radio
il parafango (paraurte) / the fender (bumper)
la routa / the tire
la luce di posizione / the tail light
la marmitta / the muffler
un guasto / the breakdown
una ruota bucata / the flat tire

OTHER BOOKS IN THE SERIES

ADVENTURES WITH SISTER PHILOMENA, SPECIAL AGENT TO THE POPE

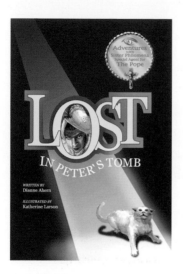

Lost in Peter's Tomb

is the first book in this series of mystery adventures. In Book One, Riley and Delaney rush to the Vatican with Sister Philomena to help the Pope with an intruder in the Apostolic Palace. A mischievous white cat leads them astray and they end up lost in Peter's tomb!

Retail Price $11.95

Break-In at the Basilica

Luigi hides in the Basilica of St Francis in Assisi, Italy, until dark. The far-off cry of a wolf sends chills down his spine. His motive for the break-in will surprise you. Walking in the foot-steps of Saints Francis and Claire, Riley and Delaney help Sister Philomena fig-ure it all out.

Retail Price $11.95

BOOK #4, *Coming soon!*

SECRETS OF SIENA

Even nuns get to take a holiday! After all of the investigations Sister Philomena has conducted recently, she needs one! *Secrets of Siena*, the next installment of *Adventures with Sister Philomena, Special Agent to the Pope*, begins with Sister Philomena taking her nephew Riley and niece Delaney to Siena, Italy, on holiday, to experience the famous Palio horse race and festival.

The Palio delivers a delight of sights, sounds, smells, fun, and excitement all by itself. However, this adventurous holiday soon turns into another exciting investigation. When the threesome visits the historic home of Saint Catherine of Siena, they discover half of an original, but until now unknown, letter written by Saint Catherine along with a thief's plans to ransom it to the Pope. The letter is invaluable to the Church because of its history, so Sister Philomena and the children must recover the rest of the letter as quickly as possible.

The clues send them off to Avignon, France and the famous Palace of the Popes. During their travels and investigation, the children learn about the history of the Church in the 1300s when the papacy was forced to flee from Rome to Avignon for safety, and Saint Catherine's role in bringing it back to Rome.

OTHER BOOKS FOUND IN
AUNT DEE'S ATTIC

Books on the Sacraments that carry the
imprimatur of the Catholic Church:

Today I Was Baptized
Today I Made My First Reconciliation
Today I Made My First Communion
Today Someone I Love Passed Away

Books for couples discerning marriage:
Today We Became Engaged

A picture book and alphabet book on Noah's Ark:
A is for Ark, Noah's Journey

Please feel free to call us at 800-352-6797 or visit us
on the web at www.auntdeesattic.com.

AUNT DEE'S ATTIC, INC.
415 Detroit Street, Suite 200
Ann Arbor, Michigan 48104